Birthday Girl

hardie grant EGMONT

Birthday Girl
first published in 2006
this edition published in 2012 by
Hardie Grant Egmont
Ground Floor, Building 1, 658 Church Street
Richmond, Victoria 3121, Australia
www.hardiegrantegmont.com.au

A CiP record for this title is available from the National Library of Australia

Text copyright © 2006 Meredith Badger
Illustration and design copyright © 2012 Hardie Grant Egmont
The moral rights of the author have been asserted

Illustration by Aki Fukuoka
Design by Michelle Mackintosh
Text design and typesetting by Ektavo

Printed in Australia by Griffin Press, an Accredited ISO AS/NZS
14001:2004 Environmental Management System printer.

5 7 9 10 8 6 4

The paper this book is printed on is certified against the
Forest Stewardship Council® Standards. Griffin Press holds
FSC chain of custody certification SGS-COC-005088. FSC
promotes environmentally responsible, socially beneficial
and economically viable management of the world's forests

Birthday Girl

by
Meredith Badger

Illustrations by
Aki Fukuoka

hardie grant EGMONT

Chapter One

Annabelle was lying on her bed, feeling terrible. She felt terrible even though it was the weekend. She felt terrible even though it was a beautiful, sunny day. And she felt terrible even though it was her birthday party.

In fact, her birthday party was the main reason she felt so bad.

I'm staying in here until it's all over and

everyone's gone home, thought Annabelle. *And I'm never,* ever *having a party again.*

Usually Annabelle loved having parties. Her birthday was in summer and she always had a party in her backyard. Each year there was a different theme.

One year it was 'Hawaiian'. Everyone wore grass skirts and long necklaces made of flowers, and they drank tropical juice out of coconut shells.

Another year the theme was 'winter' and they pretended it was really cold instead of really hot. There were huge fake icebergs on the lawn and Annabelle's Uncle Bob had made an excellent life-size snowman out of foam.

Then last year she had a 'school pool' party. Her friends all wore their school uniforms and brought their school bags. There had even been lessons ... but fun ones! In one class they made pizzas. And in another class they decorated T-shirts with glitter paint. Then they all jumped into Annabelle's pool.

So Annabelle had always been pretty sure she knew what made a good party. But that all changed the day she went to her best friend Nicole's party.

Usually Nicole had an at-home party, too. But this time she'd had it at a rock-climbing centre.

Nicole had invited the school gang — Dani, Chloe, Sarah, Lola and Annabelle. But she'd invited lots of other people, too. Most of their class went, even the boys. Some of Nicole's new basketball friends were also there.

For lunch they'd had wedges and nachos at the centre's cafe. Then Nicole's mum pulled out a big pink and gold box. Inside was a huge cake from the bakery, decorated with chocolate curls. Written on the top in pink icing was, 'Happy Birthday Nicole'. It was the most beautiful cake Annabelle had ever seen.

'This cake is awesome,' said Dani, as they each munched on a slice. 'In fact, this is one of the best parties I've ever been to. Rock-climbing is cool fun.'

'Yeah,' agreed Chloe. 'I wish we could come here for every party!'

'Was it a good party, Belly?' asked her mum when she picked her up afterwards.

'It was soooo much fun!' said Annabelle, grinning.

Then she looked at her mum. She had something to ask. It was *her* birthday soon. And she wanted her party to be just as good as Nicole's had been.

'Mum,' Annabelle said nervously, 'could I have a rock-climbing party, too?'

'I thought you liked having parties at home,' said her mum, surprised.

Annabelle felt a bit bad. She knew her mum and Uncle Bob always put a lot of

I want a party like Nic's!

effort into her parties. And until now she'd thought her parties were great. But she couldn't help feeling that Nicole's party had been heaps better. A normal backyard party suddenly seemed like something for little kids. But there was no way Annabelle could say that to her mum.

'Home parties are great, Mum,' said Annabelle, in the end. 'I just feel like doing something different this year.'

Annabelle's mum frowned. This meant she was thinking.

'OK,' she said, after a minute. 'You can have a rock-climbing party.'

'Yay!' said Annabelle, bouncing on her seat with excitement.

'Hang on,' said her mum. 'There's a *but*.'

Annabelle groaned.

Buts were never good.

'If you have a party at home you can invite whoever you want. But if you have a rock-climbing party you can only invite three people.'

'Only *three*?' said Annabelle.

That was a big *but*.

One of the reasons Nicole's party had

been so good was because there were heaps of kids there. It wouldn't be the same with just three.

But Annabelle's mum was firm.

'That's the deal,' she said. 'Now it's up to you to decide.'

Chapter Two

By Sunday, Annabelle still hadn't decided
what to do. It would be so awesome to have
a rock-climbing party. But how would she
choose who to take? There was her bestie
Nicole, for a start. Plus she had her second
besties – Sarah, Dani, Chloe and Lola.

Then there were her orchestra friends.
Annabelle had been playing in the orchestra
for a while now and she really liked Siri

and Freya. And what about the kids who lived nearby? She always invited Michiko from next door and Shae who lived down the road. Plus there was no way she could leave out Sophie, who was her friend as well as her cousin.

It was just way too hard to pick only three friends.

As Annabelle lay on her bed thinking, her mum stuck her head around the door.

'Come on, Belly. It's time for lunch at Uncle Bob's,' she said.

Annabelle and her mum had lunch at Uncle Bob's place every Sunday. Sometimes Sophie was there, too. But some Sundays she was at her mum's place.

'Cool,' said Annabelle, getting up.

She liked going to Uncle Bob's. He was an illustrator and had lots of funny drawings stuck up around the house. And this week Sophie would be there.

I can ask her what she'd do about this whole party thing, thought Annabelle. Her cousin was good at solving problems.

Sophie was using the computer when they arrived. She listened as Annabelle explained her problem.

'I think your parties are cool the way they are,' said Sophie. 'But it's up to you, I guess.' Then she typed something into the computer. 'Let's visit the Party Princess website. She might be able to help.'

Seconds later a girl appeared on the screen wearing a tiara and holding a present.

'That's the Party Princess,' explained Sophie. 'She knows everything there is to know about parties.'

Sophie clicked on the WHAT'S HOT section.

Party Princess

WHAT'S HOT RIGHT NOW?
MOCKTAIL PARTIES!

- *Wear your best clothes*
- *Serve brightly coloured soft drinks and juices in tall glasses*
- *Offer unusual snacks on silver trays*
- *Play croquet*

Annabelle grinned.

'That's it!' she said. 'I'll have a mocktail party! Then I can invite whoever I like. And it'll also be totally different to the sort of parties I usually have.'

Sophie nodded.

'Cool idea, Bell,' she said.

Over lunch, Annabelle explained her idea to her mum and Uncle Bob.

'Everyone can dress up. We can have fancy drinks in tall glasses and food on silver trays,' she said excitedly. 'Then we can all play *crock-kwit*.'

Her mum frowned for a moment. Then she laughed.

'You mean *croquet*,' she said, saying it

'croak-ay'. 'I wonder how you play it?'

Annabelle's face fell. She had hoped her mum would know.

'You're all forgetting the most important question!' said Uncle Bob suddenly. 'What sort of invitations should we make?'

Annabelle bit her lip.

Uncle Bob made Annabelle's party invitations every year. For the Hawaiian party he made girls who wiggled their hips when you pulled a tab. For the winter party he'd drawn penguins wearing sparkly hats. And for the school party he'd made invitations that looked like report cards.

But Nicole's birthday invitations had come from a proper party shop. They had gold edges and smelt like watermelon. Annabelle really wanted invitations like that this year. But before she could say anything Uncle Bob slapped the table.

'I know!' he said. 'We can make them look like cocktail glasses! And as you pull the straw the drink will disappear.'

Annabelle sighed, but very quietly. There was no way she could say anything now. Uncle Bob was way too excited.

After lunch they all set to work on the invitations. Uncle Bob designed them on the computer. Then Sophie, who was almost as good as Uncle Bob on the computer, coloured them in. Then they printed them out and everyone helped put them together. As a final touch Annabelle added red and gold glitter to the straws.

It took all afternoon but the time passed quickly. Uncle Bob kept drawing funny things in the glasses. In one he drew a dolphin wearing goggles. And in another he added a duck doing backstroke.

When the invitations were finished Sophie spread them out over the table.

'They look so cool!' she said.

Annabelle nodded.

They *did* look good. And seeing them there made her realise that her birthday was very soon! Annabelle felt all quivery just thinking about it.

This is going to be the coolest party I've ever had, she thought.

Chapter Three

'Excellent invitation, Bell!' said Sarah, a few days later. 'But how come you're not having a pool party? Your school pool party was the best.'

'I just wanted to do something different this year,' explained Annabelle. 'Pool parties are boring.'

'I don't think they're boring,' said Dani. 'Yours was awesome.'

Annabelle smiled. She thought Dani was probably just saying that to be nice.

'What should we wear?' asked Dani.

Annabelle thought for a moment.

'Something really dressy,' she replied.

'I'll borrow some clothes from my sister,' said Dani excitedly. 'She'll have something for sure.'

'Good idea,' nodded Chloe. 'What will you wear, Bell?'

Usually Annabelle wore a good top with her favourite jeans or a skirt to parties. For her school pool party she had worn her school uniform over the top of her bathers. For Nicole's rock-climbing party she'd worn leggings and a T-shirt.

But none of these things would be right for a mocktail party. She needed something really special.

'I still haven't decided yet,' Annabelle shrugged. 'But it'll be cool.'

Then she turned to Nicole.

'What about you, Nic?' she said.

But Nicole was looking at the invitation with a big frown on her face.

It's like she's not one bit excited, thought Annabelle, feeling hurt.

'The party is on the 12th?' asked Nicole, looking worried.

'Yep,' replied Annabelle. 'It starts at two o'clock. Why?'

Nicole twiddled with her ponytail. She

always did that when something was bothering her.

'Well, the Cockatoos won the semi-final,' she explained. 'So now we're in the grand final.'

Nicole had recently started playing basketball.

Annabelle gave her friend a hug.

'That's so great! But how come you look like you've just been given detention?'

Nicole sighed.

'The grand final is on the 12th.'

Annabelle stared at Nicole.

'You mean, you're not coming to my party?' she asked, her jaw dropping.

'Of *course* I'm coming,' said Nicole

Oh no!

My bestie isn't coming to my party!

quickly. 'I'll just be a bit late, that's all.'

Annabelle's heart sank.

She didn't know what to say. Nicole had been to every one of her parties since they were three. She was usually the first to arrive and the last to leave. She had always been in charge of choosing the music. And somehow she always managed to pick songs that everyone liked.

Who would do the music until she arrived?

Then there was the Happy Birthday song. Nicole always sang it the loudest. And she was the one who said, 'Hip hip!' so that everyone else could say, 'Hooray!'

If she wasn't there, would someone else remember to do it?

Just then the recess bell rang and the gang headed back to class.

Annabelle and Nicole walked side by side, but without talking. Annabelle's mind was whirling around.

Maybe I could change the party to a different day, she thought. But it was too late to do that. Most of the invitations had been sent out already.

Then Annabelle had a really horrible thought. It was so horrible that she screwed up her face and tried to shake it out of her head. But when she stopped shaking the thought was still there.

Maybe Nic doesn't want to come to my party. I bet if I was having a rock-climbing party she would miss her basketball game.

Annabelle and Nicole arrived at their classroom. Annabelle sat down, feeling terrible. Out of the corner of her eye she could see Nicole watching her. Nicole looked like she wanted to say something, but just then their teacher walked in.

'Quiet, everyone,' Mr Clarke said. 'No talking please!'

But the moment he turned around, Nicole grabbed Annabelle's hand under the desk and squeezed it tightly.

'Don't worry, Bell,' she whispered. 'After the game I'm going to change into my fastest running shoes and run the whole way to your place.'

Annabelle couldn't help smiling.

'The basketball court is about twenty blocks away from my place,' she whispered back. 'You can't run all that way!'

'Well, my dad will probably give me a lift,' admitted Nicole. 'But if we get stuck in a traffic jam I'm going to jump out and run the rest of the way. I don't want to miss any more of your party than I have to!'

'Nicole!' said Mr Clarke, turning around. 'What did I say about talking?'

'Sorry, Mr Clarke,' said Nicole.

But when he turned back she grinned at Annabelle.

'I'll be there in time for the cake,' she promised.

Annabelle grinned back. She felt much better. Of course Nicole wanted to come to her party! It was just really bad luck that the grand final was on the same day.

But at least now Annabelle was sure that her friend would get there as soon as she possibly could.

Chapter Four

After school, Annabelle had orchestra practice. Her friends Siri and Freya were already there when she arrived. Siri played the viola and Freya played cello. Annabelle played violin. She'd been learning for over a year now.

Playing in the orchestra was good fun. At the moment everyone was practising really hard because they had a concert coming up. It was at the town hall and everyone had to wear their best clothes to perform.

Annabelle had gone shopping with her mum to buy a special outfit. They bought a purple skirt with a pink ribbon around the bottom and a silky pink shirt to match. They also bought some cute shoes with bows.

Annabelle always concentrated really hard when she was playing in the orchestra. She knew all the violin parts really well because she practised them at home. But there were more things to think about when she played with everyone else. She had to follow the music on the page and

make sure she knew which bit they were up to, even when she wasn't playing. Otherwise she might miss her cue to start.

After they had played through all the pieces, Mrs Bailey clapped.

'Good work, everyone,' she said. 'The strings section sounded particularly good.'

Siri, Freya and Annabelle all grinned proudly at each other.

They were in the strings section!

During the break, Annabelle pulled out the last two party invitations.

'These are for you,' she said.

'Cool!' said Freya, looking at hers. 'I've never been to a mocktail party before. Do you still play games and stuff?'

'Um …' said Annabelle.

She hadn't really thought about the games yet. At all her other parties they had played things like musical chairs and the chocolate game.

At her school pool party they had played party games in the pool. Even pass the parcel! Annabelle's mum had wrapped each layer of the parcel in a plastic bag so it didn't get soggy. Everyone agreed afterwards that playing it in the pool was even more fun.

But Siri and Freya were a little bit older than her other friends. They might think that those games were for little kids.

Then Annabelle remembered what the Party Princess had said.

'We're going to play croquet!' she said.

Annabelle still wasn't really sure what croquet was. But it sounded like a grown-up type of game.

'Oh, and guess what?' Annabelle added. 'All the food is going to be served on silver platters!'

'How excellent!' said Siri. 'What kind of food?'

'I'm not sure yet,' admitted Annabelle. 'But it won't be anything baby-ish.'

'I can't wait!' smiled Freya. 'It sounds totally cool!'

Annabelle nodded.

'Yep, it will be,' she said.

At least, I hope it will be, she thought.

During the second part of orchestra practice, Annabelle didn't play nearly so well. She missed her cues. And she played some wrong notes, too. The problem was that her head was full of party thoughts now. Like, how was she going to find out about croquet? And what kind of food should she serve?

Then, during the final piece, Annabelle thought of something else.

What if my friends don't get along?

The same people had been coming to her parties for years. They all knew each other. But Freya and Siri had never met them before.

What if Freya and Siri don't get along with my other friends? worried Annabelle. *They are older than everyone else. And they probably like totally different music, too.*

But it was too late to change anything now. All Annabelle could do was cross her fingers and hope that everyone got along.

Chapter Five

'This afternoon I'll take you shopping for party food,' said Annabelle's mum when she dropped her off at school the next day. 'Make a list of what we'll need.'

Usually buying the party food was simple. They bought party pies, sausage rolls, cocktail frankfurts, chips and lollies. Her mum made mini-pizzas and Annabelle helped make chocolate crackles.

Sometimes they had extra things, depending on the party's theme. For the Hawaiian party there were pineapple and marshmallow skewers. For her winter party there were snowballs and rainbow icy poles. And for the school party her mum had made everyone a lunchbag with fairy bread sandwiches in them.

Then they had cake.

Annabelle's mum had a birthday cake cookbook. Every year, Annabelle spent ages choosing which one she wanted her mum to make.

For the winter party she chose the penguin cake. Annabelle's mum put blue jelly around the outside so it looked like the penguin was floating on water. When Annabelle had a farm party, her mum made a pink pig cake. She also made a batch of cupcakes and decorated them so that they looked like pigs' snouts. Everyone got their own snout to take home!

But this year Annabelle didn't want the same old party food. So at lunchtime she looked up the Party Princess site again.

THE PARTY PRINCESS SUGGESTS
- *Nori rolls*
- *Fried wontons*
- *Olives*
- *Blue cheese on mini-toast*
- *Spinach and cheese triangles*

Annabelle didn't know if she liked all of these things. *But the Party Princess is a party expert*, thought Annabelle. So she wrote all her suggestions down.

'OK, Belly,' said her mum, when Annabelle got in the car after school. 'What do we need?'

Annabelle read out her list. Her mum raised an eyebrow. 'Are you sure you want these things?' she said. 'I thought you hated olives.'

'I used to when I was little. But I'm sure I'll like them now,' said Annabelle quickly. 'And I really like nori rolls. I have them at Michiko's house all the time.'

'Maybe we can ask Michiko's mum to

help us make them?' suggested Annabelle's mum. 'And we can make the spinach and cheese triangles ourselves.'

Annabelle nodded. She liked cooking.

They parked near the bakery. In the window was a cake just like the one Nicole had at her party. Annabelle pressed her nose against the window.

I wish I could have a cake like that, she thought. But she knew her mum really liked making her birthday cakes. *I won't say anything,* decided Annabelle.

But somehow the words just blurted out anyway.

'Mum, could I have a cake from the shop this year?'

Annabelle's mum looked in the bakery window.

'Those cakes cost lots of money, Bell.'

'I know. But I want one *so* much!' said Annabelle. Then she had an idea. 'The cake can be my birthday present!' she said.

Her mum laughed.

'You don't really want a cake for a present, do you?' she said.

Annabelle nodded her head really hard and jumped up and down on the spot.

'Yes, I really, really do!'

'OK, OK!' laughed her mum. 'Let's go in and order one.'

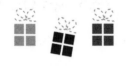

Chapter Six

The days leading up to Annabelle's party seemed to go very slowly. It was lucky that she had to practise for the concert. This kept her busy, at least.

Then one morning Annabelle woke up with a fluttery feeling in her stomach. *Why am I excited?* she wondered. And then she remembered. *That's right, it's my birthday!*

She was a year older than when she

went to bed. How weird! Annabelle lay there for a moment, trying to tell if she felt different.

She wiggled her toes. They felt the same. Then she looked at her hands. They looked exactly the same too.

But I do feel a bit different, Annabelle decided. *Like I'm a bit taller. But just on the inside, so no-one else would notice.*

Annabelle's mum came into her room, carrying a tray.

'Happy birthday, Belly!' she said, putting the tray down on the bed.

Annabelle always had breakfast in bed on her birthday.

'Yum!' said Annabelle.

It was her favourite — French toast with banana and maple syrup, and a glass of chocolate milk.

'Don't stay in bed too long,' said her mum. 'There are lots of things to do.'

Just as Annabelle finished eating, the doorbell rang.

'I'll get it!' said Annabelle, jumping up.

She was too excited to stay in bed anyway.

She opened the door. A lady was standing there, holding a pink and gold box.

'Cake for Miss Bowan,' said the lady, smiling.

'That's me!' said Annabelle, and the lady handed her the box.

Annabelle carried it carefully to the kitchen. Her mum was there, stirring a bowl full of green and white gunky stuff.

'What's that?' asked Annabelle, wrinkling her nose.

'This is the spinach and cheese mixture for the triangles,' said her mum. 'They were on your list, remember? Have you changed your mind?'

'No, no,' replied Annabelle quickly. 'I just didn't think they'd be so icky-looking.'

'They won't look icky when they're cooked,' said her mum.

Annabelle helped her mum wrap the mixture up in strips of filo pastry. Then they put them in the oven. When the first batch came out they smelt great. And they didn't look icky at all!

Then Annabelle thought of something.

She turned to her mum.

'What should we serve them on?'

The Party Princess had said the food should be served on silver platters. But Annabelle was pretty sure they didn't have any of those.

'What about these?' said her mum, smiling.

To Annabelle's surprise she was holding two large silver platters.

'They used to belong to your grandma,' explained her mum. 'They've been hiding in the cupboard for years. I think this is the perfect chance to use them again.'

The platters looked a bit old. But Annabelle's mum found some silver polish and

Annabelle scrubbed them until they shone. She had just finished when Michiko's mum, Mrs Takasaka, arrived.

Mrs Takasaka put a bamboo mat on the table. Then she got out a bag of what looked like dark green paper squares.

'This is the nori,' explained Mrs Takasaka. 'You lay it on the bamboo mat. Next you put a layer of rice on top and squash it down flat. Then you put a line of your favourite fillings in the middle. Finally, you roll it all up and cut it into pieces.'

It looked really easy when Mrs Takasaka did it. But when Annabelle tried, it wouldn't stay rolled up. And all the filling came squishing out the ends.

'Too big, maybe,' said Mrs Takasaka.

So Annabelle tried again with less filling. This time the rolls stayed together. Mrs Takasaka chopped them into discs with a very sharp knife.

'Wow!' said Annabelle. 'They look just like shop ones.'

Mrs Takasaka laughed.

'Try one. I bet ours are much tastier.'

Annabelle picked one up. She loved nori rolls. And these ones looked really good.

'Mrs Takasaka,' she said, as she munched on one, 'what is nori exactly?'

'It's a type of seaweed,' replied Mrs Takasaka.

Annabelle stared at Mrs Takasaka in

That's seaweed!

horror. Mrs Takasaka laughed when she saw Annabelle's face.

Annabelle's mum came over.

'Belly! Look at the clock!' she said. 'You'd better get ready. Your friends will be arriving soon. We'll finish up in here.'

Annabelle hurried to her bedroom. She got her blue V-neck top out of the chest of drawers, and pulled on her skirt with the beaded waistband. It was her favourite outfit. But it was the sort of thing she always wore to parties.

I need something different for this party, decided Annabelle.

She opened up her wardrobe. At first nothing looked quite right. But then she saw her new concert clothes hanging right at the back.

She felt the edge of the skirt. The material made a nice *shushing* noise between her fingers.

'I'm sure Mum won't mind if I wear

this outfit today,' Annabelle told herself.
'It's my birthday, after all!'

Then she quickly got dressed.

Just as she finished doing her hair the
doorbell rang. Annabelle looked in the
mirror. It was already a hot day and her
new clothes were quite warm. And she
would have to be careful to keep them
clean. But Annabelle didn't care.

It was absolutely the most perfect outfit
for a mocktail party.

Chapter Seven

Annabelle ran to the front door. It was Uncle Bob and Sophie. Sophie was wearing a black skirt with sequins and a red satin top. It was funny to see Sophie dressed up because she usually just wore jeans. Today she was even wearing a necklace!

'Cool outfit, Soph!' said Annabelle.

'Thanks,' said Sophie. 'I borrowed this stuff from my friend Megan.'

'What about *my* outfit?' said Uncle Bob.

Annabelle looked at him and laughed. Uncle Bob was dressed up in a tuxedo. He was even wearing a bow tie.

'You look great, too,' said Annabelle, giving him a big kiss.

Sophie handed Annabelle a parcel.

'Happy birthday!' she said.

Annabelle opened it immediately.

Inside was a double picture frame decorated with beads and shells. In one frame was a drawing of Annabelle. In the other was one of Sophie. Annabelle was poking her tongue out at Sophie. And Sophie was poking hers out at Annabelle.

Annabelle laughed.

This was how she and Sophie sometimes said hello to each other.

'I decorated the frame,' explained Sophie.

'And she did the drawings, too,' added Uncle Bob.

Annabelle went and put it on her bed-side table. Then she hugged Sophie.

'I love it so much! Thank you.'

The doorbell rang again. This time it was Chloe, Dani, Lola and Sarah. They were all wearing long, bright dresses and lots of crazy jewellery.

'Hi, guys!' she said. 'Where's Nic?' Then she felt a pang as she remembered. 'Oh yeah, that's right. She's coming later.'

For a moment, Annabelle felt a bit sad. It would be nice if Nicole was already here. But it was hard to be sad for long with her second besties around.

'Happy birthday!' they yelled excitedly, and gave Annabelle her presents.

Chloe gave her a CD and some stickers. Dani gave her a diary. Sarah and Lola gave her some green bracelets and matching hairclips.

'Thanks!' said Annabelle. 'Hey, you guys look really tall!'

Her friends grinned and lifted up their hems. They were all wobbling on shoes that were way too big.

'We borrowed my sister's stuff,'

explained Dani. 'I don't know how she could wear these shoes. They are sooo uncomfortable!'

Next to arrive were some other girls from their class. Then came Michiko and Shae. The last guests to turn up were Siri and Freya. Annabelle looked around at her friends. She almost didn't recognise them in their mocktail outfits.

'Wow, you all look so fantastic!' she grinned.

Then Uncle Bob appeared around the corner, carrying a silver tray. Balanced on top were glasses filled with brightly coloured soft drinks. Some drinks were red and pink. Some were green and blue.

A few were rainbow-striped. Each glass had a bendy straw, and some even had little umbrellas.

'Cooooool!' said everyone together.

Chloe had trouble choosing a drink.

'I don't know which one to have!' she said. 'They all look so good.'

'Don't worry, madam,' said Uncle Bob in a funny voice. 'I will be back with more.'

Chloe giggled as Uncle Bob left the room.

'The waiter called me madam!' she said.

'That's not a waiter,' laughed Annabelle. 'That's Uncle Bob!'

She tried her mocktail. It was delicious.

Then Annabelle's mum came in with

a tray of food in each hand. She raised an eyebrow when she saw that Annabelle was wearing her special concert clothes. Annabelle went red. She had a bad feeling her mum might make her get changed.

But all her mum said was, 'Be careful in those, won't you?'

'Do you have any mini-pizzas, Julia?' Dani asked Annabelle's mum.

'I hope so,' added Sarah. 'Yours are the best!'

'We've got different food this year,' explained Annabelle's mum. 'These are spinach and cheese triangles.'

Dani and Sarah both looked at them doubtfully.

'I don't really like spinach,' said Sarah.

'Annabelle,' said Dani, 'you try one first.'

Annabelle picked one up.

The triangles looked nice on the outside. They were golden brown from the oven and smelt really good.

But she kept remembering the green goopy stuff inside.

I'll just pretend it tastes nice, thought Annabelle, taking a bite.

'What's it like?' asked Sarah.

'Actually, it's delicious!' said Annabelle, surprised.

Everyone grabbed one and started munching away. Then Annabelle's mum held out the tray of nori rolls.

'These were handmade by Annabelle!' she said.

'Yum!' said Siri. 'They're my favourite!'

Everyone took one straight away.

'I bet you guys don't know what nori is,' Annabelle said as she picked one up.

'Of course we do!' said Lola and Sophie at the same time.

'Seaweed!' said Sarah.

Everyone else knows it's seaweed!

Annabelle thought she must have been the only person in the world who didn't known what nori was! She watched her friends as they helped themselves to seconds and thirds.

It wasn't long before all the triangles and nori rolls had been eaten.

Everyone is enjoying themselves, Annabelle thought happily. *This is turning out to be a great party!*

But then, quite suddenly, everything changed.

Chapter Eight

Uncle Bob came around with another tray of mocktails. Annabelle chose a rainbow one and took a big sip. This one didn't taste quite as nice as the first one. It tasted really, really sweet. Usually Annabelle loved sweet things. But this was a bit too sweet even for her.

Then she looked around at her friends. *Are they getting bored?* worried Annabelle.

I'd better put some music on!

She jumped up and went to the CD player. But what should she play?

I wish Nic was here to choose something, thought Annabelle.

Then she remembered the CD that Chloe had given her.

'Come on!' Annabelle said, as the CD came on. 'Let's dance!'

'Can we listen to something else?' complained Siri. 'I hate this CD!'

Chloe looked surprised.

'How can you hate it? It's the best!'

'I think it's dumb, too,' said Freya. 'And it's really hard to dance to.'

'It's too hot to dance anyway,' said Shae.

'Maybe we should swim instead?'

My friends are fighting! thought Annabelle. This was exactly what she had been afraid of. She wished Nicole was here. She would know what to do.

Oh, no!
My friends
are fighting!

Then Dani jumped up.

'It's easy to dance to this music,' she said. 'Just watch.'

She started doing a really funny dance.

She waved her arms around and jumped all over the place. It was so silly that everyone started laughing. And before long everyone else was dancing, too. Even Siri and Freya.

After a few songs, Dani flopped onto the couch.

'I have to stop dancing,' she said. 'I think those mocktails are turning into milkshakes in my tummy!'

'Same!' said Chloe, as she lay down on the floor.

It wasn't long before everyone else was lying down.

'My tummy keeps going *blurrrp!*' said Freya, laughing.

'Mine too!' said Lola. 'I can feel all that yummy food and too many mocktails sloshing around.'

Just then, Uncle Bob appeared.

'Would anyone like another mocktail?' he asked.

'NOOOO!' groaned everyone.

'Let's go outside,' said Sophie.

'We could play that game you told us about,' said Siri to Annabelle. 'Croaky?'

At first Annabelle wasn't sure what Siri meant. Then she realised Siri meant croquet. But Annabelle had forgotten to check what croquet was!

'Maybe we could play musical chairs instead?' she suggested.

Uncle Bob was still in the room, clearing away glasses.

'Ladies,' he said, bowing. 'Please follow me outside.'

Curiously, everyone followed him out the back door. The fresh air made Annabelle feel better straight away. Then she noticed something weird about the backyard. There were lots of little metal hoops sticking out of the ground! Leaning against the fence were wooden hammers with long handles.

'What's going on, Uncle Bob?' Annabelle whispered.

'It's a croquet set,' Uncle Bob replied. 'It's my present to you. I haven't played it for years. But I'm sure I can still remember the rules.'

'Thanks, Uncle Bob,' said Annabelle, hugging him. He was such a great uncle!

It turned out that croquet was a pretty fun game. The hammers were called mallets and you used them to hit a ball through the hoops. And Uncle Bob added a new rule. Every time you got the ball through a hoop you had to croak like a frog!

'I love this game!' said Freya.

'It's cool, isn't it?' agreed Chloe. 'But it'd be much easier without these dumb shoes on.'

They all kicked off their shoes and started playing in bare feet.

This is great! thought Annabelle happily.

Then all of a sudden Chloe screamed.

'OOOOWWWW!'

Annabelle's mum came running out of the house.

'What's happened?'

Annabelle could tell that Chloe was trying hard not to cry.

'My foot really, really hurts,' she said, with a wobbly voice.

Annabelle's mum quickly looked at Chloe's foot.

'It's a bee sting,' she said. 'You'd better sit inside and put your foot up. Everyone else wait here. It's time for the cake!'

Poor Chloe, thought Annabelle. *Bee stings really hurt!*

And to make things worse she was going to miss out on seeing the cake.

Chapter Nine

'Here it comes!' called Siri.

The back door opened and out came Uncle Bob, carrying the cake. It was decorated with candles and sparklers. Everyone sang Happy Birthday as Uncle Bob put the cake down on a fold-up table in front of Annabelle.

Usually Annabelle loved this part. But today it didn't feel quite right. It was like something was missing. Then Annabelle realised what it was.

Nicole still wasn't there!

Maybe she's decided not to come after all, thought Annabelle, disappointed.

When the singing stopped someone called out, 'Hip hip!'

'Hooray!' shouted everyone else.

'Hip hip!' said the voice again.

Annabelle looked around. It sounded like the voice was coming from over the fence. And then it was her turn to shout 'hooray', because coming through the back gate was Nicole!

Nicole was still wearing her basketball clothes. She was bright red in the face.

'Did you win?' asked Annabelle.

Nicole pulled a face.

'Well, actually … ' she said.

Annabelle's heart sank. *Poor Nic! She must have lost. What a shame!*

But then Nicole's face broke into a smile. 'We won!'

'That's so great!' said Annabelle, jumping up and down.

'Is anyone going to blow out these candles?' asked Uncle Bob. 'The cake is going to catch on fire soon!'

'Oops!' said Annabelle.

She turned around and blew out all the candles in one breath.

'Don't forget to make a wish!' said

Chloe, who had hobbled back outside.

Annabelle shut her eyes and thought about what to wish for. Usually she wished for a pony.

But today she had a different wish.

I wish it could be my birthday forever!

Annabelle's mum handed her a knife with a pink ribbon tied around the handle. As Annabelle cut the cake she was careful not to touch the bottom so her wish would come true. Then her mum cut the cake into slices and handed them around.

Nicole took a bite of hers.

'Hey, this is like the cake I had at my party!' she said.

'It's from the same bakery,' explained Annabelle. 'It's so yum, isn't it?'

'It *is* yum,' agreed Nicole. 'But the ones your mum makes are even better.'

'Yeah,' said Michiko. 'Your mum's cakes rock. I love all the cool shapes and colours she makes them.'

'Me too,' said Lola. 'I always love your invitations, too. I've kept all of them!'

Annabelle stared at her friends. She

was too surprised to say anything. Did everyone like her old parties after all?

'I thought … ' she started to say.

But Annabelle didn't get to finish her sentence because suddenly Sophie yelled, 'Look out!'

Annabelle spun around.

The fold-up table the cake was sitting on was starting to collapse!

'Oh, no!' cried Annabelle.

She rushed forward to catch the cake before it fell. But before she got there she tripped on a rock and fell flat on her face.

A second later the cake toppled off the table. It fell with a splat beside her.

'Are you OK?' asked Michiko, helping Annabelle up.

Annabelle looked down at her clothes. There was a big grass stain on her shirt and a rip in her skirt. And birthday cake everywhere!

When Mum sees my concert clothes I'm going to be in big trouble, thought Annabelle, her eyes blurry with tears.

That was when Annabelle decided she'd had enough of this party. Everything was meant to be perfect on your birthday. But things just kept going wrong.

Annabelle ran into the house and into her bedroom. She got changed and then flopped down on her bed.

It was strange. Not long ago she had wished that her birthday would last forever. Now she just wanted it to be over.

Chapter Ten

Annabelle's violin was in its case next to her bed. She picked it up. Playing music always made her feel better. But today it only helped a bit. Definitely not enough to want to go back outside.

After she had been playing for a while there was a knock on her door.

'Can I come in?' asked her mum.

Annabelle looked at her concert clothes

crumpled up on the floor. She didn't want her mum to see that she had ruined them. But there was no point hiding them. Her mum would find out in the end.

'OK,' said Annabelle.

Her mum came in and sat beside her.

'You are playing so well, Belly,' she said. 'I can't wait to hear you at the concert.'

'I won't be able to play,' said Annabelle sadly.

'Why not?' asked her mum, surprised.

'Because I've wrecked my concert clothes,' admitted Annabelle, showing her.

Annabelle's mum looked at the grass stain and the tear.

'You know, these aren't too bad. I think that grass stain will come out. And I can sew up that tear so you won't even know it's there. Besides,' she added. 'You have to play at the concert so you can wear this.'

She handed Annabelle a small blue box with a purple ribbon tied around it.

Annabelle was confused.

'But I thought the cake was my present,' she said.

'This isn't really a birthday present,'

explained her mum. 'It's to show how proud I am that you're about to play in your first concert.'

Annabelle opened the box.

Inside was a small silver treble clef, hanging on a chain.

'It's so beautiful!' said Annabelle. 'Can I wear it today or do I have to wait for the concert?'

'You can wear it today,' her mum laughed. 'Put it on and then come with me. There's something else you should see.'

Annabelle followed her mum into the kitchen. All her friends were crowded around the kitchen table.

'What's going on?' asked Annabelle.

Her friends all stepped to the side. Annabelle couldn't believe it. There on the table was a brand new birthday cake! It was shaped like a castle with lots of pointy turrets.

'Do you like it?' asked Nicole. 'We made

it out of ice-cream! And the turrets are ice-cream cones.'

'Yeah, what do you think?' said Chloe. 'Is it as good as the other one?'

Annabelle looked at the cake. It was already starting to melt. On the side some-one had written, 'Happy Birthday, Bell!' in chocolate dots. Some of the letters were much bigger than the others.

Annabelle looked at her friends.

'Are you kidding?' she said. 'It's *way* better than the other one!'

'Hey!' said Nicole. 'This means we can sing Happy Birthday again. But let's sing it the other way this time.'

As she started singing, everyone else

joined in. Even Annabelle's mum!

Happy birthday to you

You live in the zoo

You look like a monkey

And you smell like one too!

When the song finished, everyone cheered again. And this time it was even louder than before.

'Let's eat the cake!' said Annabelle.

Then she grabbed one of the turret-cones and used it to scoop up some of the ice-cream castle.

'Cool!' giggled Sarah, reaching out for a turret.

Before long everyone else was licking a turret, too.

'How about a swim?' suggested Lola.

'Great idea,' agreed Sophie, starting to head outside. Then she stopped. 'Hang on … None of us have our bathers.'

'Wait there!' said Annabelle, dashing out of the room.

She ran to her bedroom and grabbed as many T-shirts as she could find. Five minutes later, everyone was in the pool. Annabelle couldn't stop laughing. It was so funny to see everyone swimming around in her clothes.

Nicole swam up to her.

'I wish I'd been here from the start,' she said. 'Everyone keeps telling me what a great party it's been.'

Annabelle was surprised. She hadn't thought the party was very good at all. But then she thought about the day. A few bad things had happened. Like Chloe getting a bee sting. And the cake getting wrecked. But there had been lots of good things, too.

She looked around at everyone playing in the pool. Sophie and Michiko were both trying to sit on the li-lo, but they kept falling off. Dani was teaching the others her crazy dance. It looked even crazier in the water.

'I guess it *has* been pretty good,' said Annabelle, smiling. 'But I wonder what the Party Princess would say about it?'

'Who cares what *she* thinks?' Nicole sang out. 'You know more about parties than she does, any day!'